Dragons
of Krad

Don't miss the other adventures
of Darek and Zantor:

The Dragonling
A Dragon in the Family
Dragon Quest

Coming soon:

Dragon Trouble
Dragons and Kings

The DRAGONLING

Dragons of Krad

By Jackie French Koller

Illustrated by Judith Mitchell

ALADDIN
New York   London   Toronto   Sydney   New Delhi

This book is a work of fiction. Any references to historical events, real people, or real places are used fictitiously. Other names, characters, places, and events are products of the author's imagination, and any resemblance to actual events or places or persons, living or dead, is entirely coincidental.

ALADDIN

An imprint of Simon & Schuster Children's Publishing Division
1230 Avenue of the Americas, New York, New York 10020
This Aladdin paperback edition April 2019
Text copyright © 1997 by Jackie French Koller
Cover illustration copyright © 2019 by Tom Knight
Interior illustrations copyright © 1997 by Judith Mitchell
Also available in an Aladdin hardcover edition.
All rights reserved, including the right of reproduction in whole
or in part in any form.
ALADDIN and related logo are registered trademarks
of Simon & Schuster, Inc.
For information about special discounts for bulk purchases,
please contact Simon & Schuster Special Sales at 1-866-506-1949
or business@simonandschuster.com.
The Simon & Schuster Speakers Bureau can bring authors to
your live event. For more information or to book an event contact
the Simon & Schuster Speakers Bureau at 1-866-248-3049 or visit
our website at www.simonspeakers.com.
Designed by Laura Lyn DiSiena
The text of this book was set in ITC New Baskerville.
Manufactured in the United States of America 0319 OFF
2 4 6 8 10 9 7 5 3 1
Library of Congress Control Number 2018958558
ISBN 978-1-5344-0071-9 (hc)
ISBN 978-1-5344-0070-2 (pbk)
ISBN 978-1-5344-0072-6 (eBook)

To my brother Jim, with love

Dragons
of Krad

Prologue

WHEN DAREK RESCUED A BABY dragon and brought it home to his village, he dreamed of a bright new tomorrow where dragons and Zorians could live together as friends. And indeed, after a difficult beginning, Darek and his dragon friend, Zantor, did win the hearts of the villagers.

But Darek didn't count on the jealousy of the other Zorian children. Rowena, daughter of the

Chief Elder, grew to love Zantor deeply. When Darek refused to allow her to play with Zantor, Rowena begged her father for a dragonling of her own. This wish sparked a dragonquest that ended in tragedy. Darek's best friend, Pola, along with Zantor and three other Great Blue dragonlings were lost when a runaway wagon carried them into the dreaded Black Mountains of Krad.

Filled with grief and rage, Darek confronted Rowena and blamed her for the tragedy. Determined to right the wrongs she had done, Rowena slipped away in the night on a quest to find Pola and the dragons. When Darek discovered that she was headed for the Black Mountains, he followed, bent on stopping her. But Rowena would not be stopped. Instead she helped Darek see that they shared the blame for the tragedy.

Now the two have discovered that they share something else—the ability to communicate with Zantor. While they are arguing, a mind message comes from the dragonling—a cry for help. Putting aside past differences, Darek and Rowena set off on a new quest. Together they venture into the Black Mountains, risking everything to find their friends.

1

DARK MISTS SWIRLED AROUND Darek as he made his way up a narrow pass into the Black Mountains of Krad. Rowena, daughter of the Zorian Chief Elder, followed a few steps behind. The mist felt damp against Darek's skin, and the stench of it made him gag. It smelled like rotted burning flesh, and that worried him.

Darek heard a cough and looked back over his shoulder.

"Are you all right?" he asked.

"Yes." Rowena nodded. "I'm getting tired, though. My eyes sting, and it's hard to breathe."

"Shall we rest awhile?" Darek asked.

"No. Pola and Zantor may be in danger. We've got to keep going."

Darek nodded. He could hear the mind cries too. His dragon friend, Zantor, was sending messages of distress. Zantor and Darek's best friend, Pola, had disappeared into the Black Mountains more than a week ago. They and three other Great Blue dragonlings had been carried off by a runaway wagon. Darek and Rowena felt responsible. They had been jealous of each other and had quarreled over Zantor. As a result, the Chief Elder had ordered his men to capture another dragonling for Rowena. While on the dragonquest, Pola, Zantor, and the others had been lost.

Rowena coughed again and gasped for air.

"Pull your collar up over your mouth and nose," Darek said. "The cloth will filter some of the smoke."

Strange shapes loomed out of the mist. Black rocks, like cinders, dotted their path. All Darek's senses were alert, keen to the dangers that might assail them at any moment.

"I wonder what our families will think when they wake this morning and find us gone," he said quietly.

Rowena didn't answer right away.

"We must not think of that," she said at last. "We must dream of the day when we return with Pola and the dragons."

Darek wished he could be sure that day would come, but he could not. No one had ever returned from the Black Mountains of Krad. For centuries now, it had been forbidden even to venture into them. What would his parents and his older brother, Clep, think when they realized where he had gone? He could see his mother's tearstained face now.

We will find a way back, Mother, he promised silently.

"Did you hear that?" Rowena suddenly cried out.

Darek stopped and listened. He thought he heard a soft scuffling sound, but when he peered into the mist, all he could make out were strange, twisted rock forms and the stumps of long-dead trees. "I don't see anything," he whispered.

"No," Rowena said. "I guess not." She put her hand to her forehead and moaned softly.

"Ooohh," she said. "My head and stomach ache."

Darek's head hurt too. Could the very mists be poisonous? he wondered.

"We're almost to the peak," he told Rowena. "It will be easier going down the other side. We won't have to breathe as hard."

The ground beneath them leveled off at long last, and they started to descend. Darek began to move with greater caution. If something or someone was waiting below, he wanted to see it before it saw him. His headache was worse, making it harder and harder to think. Behind him, he heard Rowena moan once more.

"Are you sure you're all right?" he asked again.

"Yes," she said, but her voice trembled.

Darek's worry deepened. He had to get her

out of the mountains quickly. "Can you walk any faster?" he asked.

"I—I don't know. I can't even think straight."

Darek turned. Rowena's skin was very pale, and her lips looked blue.

"Lean on me," he said.

Rowena gladly took his arm, and they struggled on together. Darek shook his head. It felt as if the mist were seeping into his mind. Minutes seemed to drag by. Rowena was leaning on him more and more heavily.

"Is it much farther?" she asked weakly.

"No, not much. See, the mist is thinning."

"Good, because I don't feel . . . ooohh." Rowena suddenly pushed Darek aside, clapped a hand over her mouth, and started to run.

Darek stumbled on a cinder and fell. "Rowena,

wait!" he cried. He scrambled to his feet again, but before he could catch her, Rowena disappeared into the mist.

"Rowena!" he called, but there was no reply, only a distant retching sound.

Then, suddenly, there was a scream.

2

DAREK FOUGHT THE URGE TO RUN in the direction of the scream. Instead he moved cautiously, stealing from rock to rock. If someone, or something, had caught Rowena, he had to be careful. It would do neither of them any good if he got captured too. The mist had cleared a little, and he could begin to see something of Krad. It was a bleak, colorless place, with runty, withered trees and stubby brown grasses.

A movement below caught his eye, and he strained to see.

Rowena!

His friend had reached the plateau at the foot of the mountains. There she was surrounded by a number of bent little creatures that hopped about her excitedly. They were chanting over and over in high, flutelike voices.

"A pretty!" they cried. "A pretty! A pretty!"

Rowena hugged her arms around her like a frightened child. "Go away! Go away!" she cried. "Leave me alone!"

Before long, there was another sound—hooves pounding in the distance. Darek looked toward the horizon and saw a group of riders thunder up over the lip of the plateau. The riders were broad and tall, with dark hooded

capes. They were mounted on long-haired white yukes, much like the ones back in Zoriak, only larger. As the riders bore down on Rowena, the little bent creatures around her shrieked and scurried away.

One of the smaller ones was too slow. A whip lashed out from the hand of one of the riders and stung it with a fierce blow on the leg. The creature yelped and scrabbled into the brush. The rider threw his head back and laughed. His hood fell away, and Darek saw a face that was human-like but covered in fur.

A Kraden!

A chill crept up Darek's back. Back in Zoriak, he had heard stories of Kradens—big, hairy men who had supposedly driven the Zorians out of Krad long ago. Darek had always thought they were just old tales. But these Kradens were real—living and breathing! Poor Rowena looked terrified.

"Who are you?" one of the Kradens demanded.

"Rowena," she answered in a trembling voice.

"Why have you come here?" the man asked.

Rowena seemed at a loss to answer.

Darek felt confused too. Why *had* they come there? Had the mist addled his mind? Why couldn't he remember?

Then he heard a sound deep inside his head. *Rrronk!* Yes! Zantor. Zantor and Pola. That was why they had come. He must keep focused on that.

Rowena must have heard the mind cry too. "My friends!" she said suddenly. "They're in trouble. I've come to help them."

"Have you, now?" The men looked at one

another and chuckled. "And how is a slip of a girl like you going to help anyone?"

Rowena drew herself up and tossed her head. "I'm stronger than I look," she announced.

At this, all the men burst out laughing.

"That's good news," one of them said, "because we've plenty of work for you to do."

Rowena crossed her arms. "Work?" she said. "I'll not work for you. I'm the daughter of the Chief Elder."

"Are you, now?" another Kraden asked. "Well, then, we'll have to find you a jewel-handled broom, won't we?"

With another loud laugh, the Kradens swooped forward, and one of them scooped Rowena up, pulling her into his saddle.

"Come, lads," he said. "Let's take *Her Highness*

to visit old Jazee." Then he and the others turned their yukes around and thundered away.

Darek stared after them. Who was old Jazee? he wondered. And what did the man mean when he said there was plenty of work to do? It did not bode well.

Darek decided to try to keep his own presence a secret until he could learn more. Slowly he crept down the mountainside until he reached the place where Rowena had been captured. He noticed a trail of dark droplets among the footprints and remembered the small creatures and the lash of the whip. Suddenly he heard a high, thin cry.

Gleeep. Gleeep.

Darek's head jerked around. The wounded creature was lying beside a nearby rock, nursing its leg. It caught sight of him and scrambled to

get away, but it was only able to move a few steps before collapsing again.

"Gellp!" it cried.

Darek frowned. He had no time to help a wounded . . . whatever. He started to walk away, but his conscience would not let him. Quickly he pulled his shirt out of his britches and tore a strip from the hem. Then he unfastened the waterskin from his belt and squirted a little into the dirt at his feet, mixing a muddy paste. Taking a handful of the paste, he approached the creature. It shrank back, staring at him with huge yellow-green eyes.

"I won't hurt you," Darek soothed. "I just want to help." He knelt beside the creature and gently straightened its leg.

"Gellp!" it cried again.

"Sorry," Darek said. "This should make you feel better." The creature was the size of a young child, with scaly gray skin. It looked almost like a cross between a dragon and a human. Darek couldn't help feeling kindly toward it. He packed the healing mud over the wound, then gently bandaged the leg.

"There," Darek said, getting to his feet again. "If you stay off it for a day or two, you should be fine."

The creature turned and pointed a knobby finger toward the road. "Your pretty?" it asked.

Darek looked down the road too. There was no sign of Rowena or the men now. "No," he answered. "She's not my pretty. But she's my friend. Do you know where they've taken her?"

"Zahr take pretty," the creature said.

"Zahr?" Darek said. "Who's Zahr?"

The creature gave a little cough. "Zahr, king," it said hoarsely.

Darek stared again at the empty road. "Where did Zahr take pretty?" he asked.

"Prison," the creature said.

Darek whirled around. "Prison! What do you mean, prison?"

The creature cringed. "Go now," it said, scrambling away.

"No, wait." Darek took a breath to calm himself. "Please tell me more about the prison," he pleaded.

The creature coughed again. "Go now," it repeated. And then, almost magically, it disappeared.

"Hey, wait!" Darek called after it. "One more question, please! Have you seen another Zorian, like me, or a small blue dragon?"

"Zahhhr," came the faint, choked reply.

3

DARTING FROM TREE TO SCRUBBY
tree, Darek slowly made his way across the plateau.
The mist was thinner now, and his head seemed
to be clearing. In the distance, he heard fearful
roaring sounds. Cautiously he approached the
lip where he had first seen the Kradens. He got
down on his belly, inched forward, and peered
out across the valley. A large rambling village
stretched in front of him. It had a grim look to it.

A gray, smoke-stained castle stood at its center. This was surrounded by smaller houses and hundreds of squat stone hovels. The mist, though thin, hung over everything. Suddenly Darek heard a roar just below him. He looked down, and his breath caught in his throat.

"Zatz!" he swore softly.

There at the base of the plateau was a huge cage, nearly half the size of the town. Great creatures milled about in it, roaring and belching flame at one another.

Red Fanged dragons!

Darek had never seen a Red Fanged dragon before. The last one in Zoriak had been killed long before he was born. He knew all about them from legends, though. They were not red, as their name might suggest, but pearly white. Quite beautiful,

actually, were it not for the vicious red fangs that gave their mouths the look of dripping blood. It was not just their looks that made them fearsome, though. They were also huge, second only in size to the Great Blues. And they were flesh lovers. Reds dined mostly on other dragons, but in Zoriak they had been known to raid the village from time to time.

Darek shuddered at the thought. He stared down at the cage again. How much meat must it take to satisfy the appetites of so many Red Fanged dragons? he wondered. Portions of charred dragon skeletons lay strewn about the pen, and a steady stream of smoke rose up from it. Red Fanged dragons always flamed their prey alive before eating it. So this was the source of the mist, Darek suddenly realized. Dragonsbreath!

Why would the Kradens keep these beasts? he wondered.

"Well, well!" A loud voice startled Darek. "What have we here?"

Darek looked up and saw a dark hooded figure towering over him. He started to scramble to his knees, but something hard and sharp dug into his back and pressed him to the dirt.

"Not so fast, Zorian!" the voice commanded.

Darek slowly twisted to get a better look at the figure. A thick metal-encrusted boot was planted near his shoulder. Darek's gaze followed it up. A large furry-faced man stared down at him.

"State your name and mission," the man snarled.

Darek tried to keep his voice from trembling. "Darek," he said. "Darek of Zoriak. Some . . . some of my friends fled into these mountains a few days back. I . . . I'm only trying to find them."

The Kraden laughed. "Another one?" he asked. "What sorts of fools are the Zorians raising these days?"

Darek did not answer.

"Well," the Kraden said, "no matter. Fresh blood is always welcome here."

The Kraden lifted the lance from between Darek's shoulders and plunged it into the dust not a finger's breadth from his nose.

"On your feet!" he bellowed.

Darek scrambled to do as he was told. He stood straight and tall. Still, he only came up to the man's middle.

The Kraden glared down at him, pulling on his hairy chin. "How old are you?" he asked.

"A Decanum," Darek said.

The Kraden shook his head and swore. "Too young for the mines," he grumbled. "You any good with dragons?"

"Yes, sir," Darek said, swallowing hard again. "But . . . I don't plan to stay."

At this, the Kraden threw his head back and roared. He laughed until tears rolled down his furry cheeks. Then he slapped his leg and laughed some more.

"Don't plan to stay . . . ," he repeated breathlessly when at last he could speak again. "That's a good one, lad. A good one indeed."

Then his eyes narrowed, and his lips twisted into a sneer. "No one ever leaves Krad," he growled.

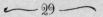

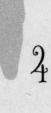

2

CASTLE KRAD WAS AS DARK AND forbidding up close as it had looked from afar. Darek stared at its twisted, smoke-stained battlements.

"Is that where Zahr lives?" he asked.

The Kraden's eyes narrowed.

"Where did you hear the name of Zahr?" he asked.

"A little creature told me," Darek said, "back

on the mountain. He said Zahr had taken my friends."

The Kraden's brows crashed together. "Blasted Zynots," he swore. "What else did they tell you?"

Darek shook his head. "Nothing," he said.

The Kraden eyed him suspiciously. "Well, no matter," he said. "That's all you'll remember soon enough—nothing." He pushed open the heavy door of a low stone house and motioned Darek inside.

It was steamy and dark inside and smelled of medicines and herbs. It took a few moments for Darek's eyes to adjust to the dimness. Then he was able to make out an old cronelike woman bent over the hearth.

"Another customer for you, Jazee," the man said.

The woman looked up in surprise. "Another?" she said. "That's three in a fortnight!"

Darek's ears perked up. Three! He and Rowena were two. The third must have been Pola!

"Aye." The man nodded. "This one thinks he's here on holiday. Told me he's not staying."

The crone cackled. "Jazee will cure him of that," she said. She picked up one of her vials and

poured a few drops of green liquid into a carved stone cup. "Drink up, boy," she said.

Darek pressed his lips tight and turned away.

"Do as Jazee says," the man growled. He grabbed Darek and pulled his mouth open. The crone poured the liquid down Darek's throat. It burned and made him gag. When he looked at the woman again, he felt light-headed and dizzy. He tried to look away, but her eyes held his fast.

"Tell me who you are," she commanded.

"Darek," Darek mumbled. The woman's face wavered and swam before his eyes.

"Darek who?" the crone asked.

Darek searched inside his head for an answer, but his mind was nothing but a vast, empty cave. "I . . . don't know."

The woman smiled. "You are Darek of Krad,"

she told him, "prisoner to the Kingdom of Zahr. From your past life, you will remember only the things that are of use to us here. Go now with Org, and do as you are commanded."

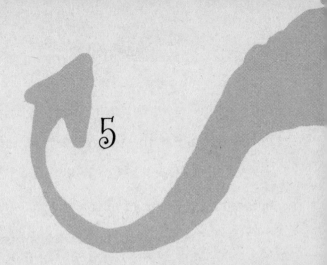

5

DAREK FOLLOWED ORG THROUGH
narrow, twisted, foul-smelling streets. Kraden
children hissed and spat at him. Women leaned
out of the doorways and called him names like
"dragon-wit" and "fang-breath." It was a relief to
reach the pastures at the far side of town at last.
Vast numbers of dragons grazed there, but not the
Red Fangs. They were kept in their cage on the
outskirts of the village. Darek recognized some of

the dragons—Green Horned, Yellow Crested, and Purple Spotted. Others were new to him.

"You'll know all there is to know of dragons before long," Org told him.

Darek was not unhappy at this prospect. The dragons were far more pleasant, it seemed, than the people of Krad. But why were the great creatures content to stay among such men?

"Why don't the dragons just fly away?" he asked Org.

"They can't," Org told him. "We bind their wings when they're young, until their flight muscles wither. You'll see soon enough. Come. Might as well get you started."

Darek followed Org into a long, low building. It was a combination stable and nursery for the dragons, as well as a dormitory for the prisoners who tended them. A number of prisoners were hard at work mucking out the dragon stalls. They looked up when Darek and Org came in. Darek felt an immediate kinship with them. The prisoners were not large and furry like the Kradens. They looked much like Darek and seemed close to him in age too. The prisoners paused and stared as Darek and Org passed, but the crack of an overseer's whip quickly returned them to their duties.

"Got a new one for you, Daxon," Org said, pushing Darek toward another Kraden.

The man named Daxon seemed pleased. "Three in a fortnight," he said, raising his eyebrows. "To what do we owe this good fortune?"

Org shrugged. "Word must be spreading about the pleasures of life here in Krad."

Daxon roared with laughter over this joke.

Org grabbed Darek by the collar and shoved him in front of Daxon. "Bow," he said, pushing Darek to his knees. "Daxon is master of the stock-yards, your master now too. You will call him 'master' when you speak to him, and you will obey his orders without question." Then he let Darek go and turned to face Daxon.

"His name is Darek," he said. "Jazee probed his thoughts. She says he should be a natural with dragons. Rebellious by nature, though, so don't spare the whip."

Daxon laughed. "When have you ever known me to spare the whip, my friend?" He looked down at Darek, pulling at the fur on his chin. "Rebellious, huh?" he said slowly. "Well, we'll just have to see to it that you're too tired to rebel, won't we?" Daxon looked over toward the other prisoners. "Pola!" he shouted. "Come here!"

One of the prisoners dropped his rake and hurried over. Darek couldn't help noticing how thin and tired the boy looked. His hands were all raw and blistered. The prisoner bowed to Daxon.

"Yes, Master?" he said.

"Take this new prisoner, and teach him everything you've learned. Start in the nursery. No supper for either of you until the pens are cleaned, the dragonlings fed, and the newborns wingbound."

Pola's face fell. "Yes, Master," he whispered, bowing again. Then to Darek he said, "Follow me."

Darek rose to follow, but suddenly Daxon's hand flew out and boxed his ear. "Bow!" he thundered.

Darek quickly dipped his head. "Yes, Master," he mumbled.

"That's better," Daxon said. "Never enter or leave my presence without bowing!"

Darek bowed once more, just to be safe, then turned and silently followed Pola.

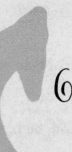

6

A MILLION QUESTIONS RACED through Darek's mind as he followed Pola along the corridor to the nursery. He hoped he and this prisoner boy would have a chance to talk privately. Maybe Pola could help him understand what was happening to him.

"Here," Pola said. He took a rake down from a hook on the wall and handed it to Darek. Then he pushed a door open and motioned Darek through.

The air inside was warm and damp and filled with the chirpings and callings of young dragons. Darek couldn't help smiling at the colorful creatures tumbling and playing on the nursery floor. He noticed a little cluster of Blues huddled together, sleeping, on the far side of the room. His smile broadened. They were so beautiful, even as babies. But the bandages wound tightly around their silvery wings saddened Darek.

"How long do they have to wear those things?" he asked.

"Half an anum," Pola said tiredly. "Until their wing muscles shrink beyond repair."

"Why don't the Kradens want them to fly?" Darek asked.

"They're easier to manage this way," Pola said.

"Who *are* these Kradens?" Darek began. "And why—"

"Look," Pola interrupted. "We've got a lot of work ahead of us if we want to eat."

Just then, Darek heard a commotion. He looked and saw that one of the little Blues had awakened. It was struggling to make its way through the maze of other dragons toward Darek and Pola.

"Thrummm!" Darek could hear it singing as it got closer. *"Thrummm, thrummm, thrummm."* Darek could have sworn its big green eyes were looking right at him.

Pola frowned. "That dratted Blue," he said. "Too darn friendly for its own good."

The Blue dragon kept making little hops in a sad attempt to fly. But that, of course, was impossible. At last, it hurled itself through the air and

smacked with a thud into Darek's chest. Both of them tumbled to the ground.

"Thrummm," the dragonling sang. *"Thrummm, thrummm, thrummm."* Then *thwip, thwip!* Out flicked its forked tongue, covering Darek with tickly kisses.

Darek twisted and rolled, laughing until his stomach hurt.

"Stop it! Hey!" he begged. "What's wrong with you, you silly thing?" He finally managed to push the beast off and get back to his feet. Still, the creature kept dancing around him, butting him and nuzzling his chest.

"He seems to want something in your jerkin pocket," Pola said.

"There isn't anything in my pocket," Darek said. He put his arms up to fend off another nuzzle.

"He sure seems to think there is," Pola said.

"Well, there isn't," Darek insisted. But he felt his pocket just to be sure.

There *was* something there. Darek reached in and pulled out several hard, white lumps.

"*Thrummm,*" sang the little dragon. It gobbled the lumps before Darek even got a good look at them.

"What were they?" Pola asked.

"I don't know," Darek said. "But *he* sure seemed to know. I wonder how?"

Pola shrugged. "Smell?"

Darek shook his head. "Dragons don't have much sense of smell."

The little dragon nuzzled Darek's pocket once more. "Sorry, pal," Darek said with a laugh. "I don't have any more." He rubbed the budding horns on the dragon's head.

"I wouldn't do that if I were you," Pola warned.

"Do what?" Darek asked.

"Get too friendly with him. It'll just make it harder in the end."

"In the end?" Darek repeated. "What do you mean?"

"When they feed him to the Red Fangs," Pola said.

Darek's breath caught in his throat. "What?" he whispered hoarsely.

"Didn't they tell you?" Pola asked quietly. "That's what they raise them for."

7

DAREK AND POLA SAT STARING AT
the empty table in front of them. Darek's stomach
was hollow and aching, and his blistered hands
stung. He and Pola hadn't finished their chores
fast enough to suit Daxon.

"I'm sorry I wasn't faster," Darek said. "This is
my fault."

Pola waved his words away. "I didn't finish in

time my first day, either," he said. "You'll be faster tomorrow."

And Darek would, he vowed, if it killed him. Pola would not have to go hungry another day on his account.

"Wench! More slog!" Daxon yelled from a nearby table.

A young girl, around Darek's age, made her way among the tables. She was balancing a heavy tray of foaming mugs.

"Faster!" Daxon bellowed.

"I'm moving as fast as I can!" the girl snapped. She reached Daxon and banged a mug down in front of him. Flecks of foam splashed up into his face. Daxon grabbed her wrist and glared into her eyes. She glared back. Darek held his breath, wondering what would happen next.

Daxon began to laugh. "Spirit!" he said, releasing her wrist. "I like a wench with spirit. Too bad you Zorians are so ugly."

The girl whirled and stomped away, and Daxon and his friends had another laugh.

Ugly? Darek thought. He saw nothing ugly about the girl. He thought her quite beautiful, in fact. And he also admired her spirit.

"What is a Zorian?" he asked Pola.

"We are Zorians," Pola said. "At least, that's what the Kradens call us."

"Are all . . ."

"No more questions." Pola put a finger to his lips and nodded toward Daxon, who was eyeing them suspiciously. "We are forbidden to speak of anything but our work."

✳   ✳   ✳

Darek's tiny cell of a room was cold and dark. The walls were rough gray stone, and there was one small barred window. He shivered as he lay on his pallet, a threadbare blanket clutched tightly around him. His body was exhausted, but his mind was even more tired. All day, he'd been straining to remember who he was, where he had come from. But the effort had given him nothing more than a pounding headache.

Darek's thoughts were suddenly interrupted by a soft scraping noise. He sat up, clutching his blanket close.

One of the large stones in the wall near the floor was moving!

As Darek watched, the stone slid slowly into the room, and a face appeared. A body followed the face, and then another. Soon four boys and two girls

had crawled into the room. Pola was among them, and so was the girl who had spilled slog on Daxon.

The boy who had been first to appear pressed a finger to his lips in warning. "I am Arnod," he whispered. "We come in friendship."

"What if they find you here?" Darek asked.

Arnod snorted softly. "They'll feed us all to the Red Fangs," he said.

Darek's eyes widened, but Arnod waved his worries away. "They won't find us," he said. "Daxon and his men drink themselves into a stupor every night. They have no knowledge of our meetings."

One of the girls smiled. "They think us simple-minded fools," she added. "It suits our purpose to let them believe that."

Darek nodded his understanding, and the prisoners sat down cross-legged around his pallet. They told him their names, and the one named Arnod leaned forward.

"You and Rowena are new," Arnod said, nodding toward the girl who had spilled the slog. "And Pola arrived just last week. There must be a connection. What can you tell us of who you are or how you came here?"

Darek sighed and slowly shook his head. "I remember nothing," he whispered.

"Nor I," Rowena added.

The faces of Arnod and the others fell.

"I'm sorry," Darek said.

"It's all right," Arnod said. "It was the same with Pola. It has always been the same. We were hoping you might be from Zoriak. But we aren't even sure such a place exists anymore. . . ."

"Zoriak?" Darek repeated. "What is Zoriak?"

Arnod sighed. "It is a long story. Our legends tell us that this valley was once called Zor. It was peaceful and beautiful then, and the mountains that ringed it were green and full of life. Only Zorians lived here."

"What happened?" Rowena asked.

"The Kradens came, from Beyond. They were bigger and stronger. They conquered most of us and made us prisoners, but a few Zorians escaped over the mountains. In the Long Ago, some of them would come back and try to help us escape too. They talked of a land they had named Zoriak, which means 'New Zor.' They said we could live there in freedom. But few of those escapes succeeded, and then the mountains died. Those who came after that, like you, knew nothing of Zoriak."

"How did the mountains die?" Darek asked.

"The dragonsbreath," Arnod explained. "For some reason, it clings to the mountain peaks, killing everything."

"If the Red Fangs are the cause of the dragons-breath," Rowena said, "why do the Kradens breed them?"

"They love blood sport," Arnod said. "They compete to raise the biggest and fiercest dragons. Then they pit them against one another and wager on the outcomes. The Kradens use them in battle too. King Zahr is at war with his brother, Rebbe, whose kingdom lies south of the Great Plain of Krad."

Darek's eyes widened. "King Zahr makes war against his own brother?"

"Yes." Arnod nodded. "They had a falling-out long ago over a prize Red Fang. They have been at war ever since."

"This Zoriak," said Rowena. "Has anyone ever gone in search of it?"

Arnod shook his head. "No. The Kradens have no interest in the place. Besides, they cannot tolerate the dragonsbreath in the mountains. It is poison to them in such density. Zorians tolerate it better, but it addles their brains."

It was all too much. Darek's head was growing heavy from the talk. He was even starting to hear strange sounds, like dragon whimpers, in his ears. He caught Rowena's eye and saw that she looked as tired and confused as he.

Pola reached out and clapped them each on the arm. "Enough talk for one night, friends," he said. "We will speak of these things again soon. For now, you must sleep."

8

THE NEXT DAY, DAREK WORKED AT a furious pace. He refused to give in to his hunger or fatigue, refused to pay heed to his swollen hands or aching back. There would be dinner tonight, he was sure. He was keeping right up with Pola, despite the annoying little Blue. The dragonling still kept butting him playfully and darting in to give him quick licks on the cheek.

"Go away!" Darek shouted repeatedly. At times,

he gave the little beast a gentle shove or raised his arm to block its advances.

"*Rrronk,*" the little creature would whimper. Darek had no intention of encouraging it in any way, though. He had enough to worry about without getting attached to a Red Fang's dinner.

"Persistent, isn't he?" Pola remarked.

"Yes." Darek frowned. "Why doesn't he bother you? Why is it just me?"

Pola shrugged. "He used to hang around me, until you arrived. But he was nowhere near as affectionate with me. It's almost like he knows you."

Darek felt a little prickle run up his spine. He stared at the dragon. "Maybe he does," he said softly. "Remember that pocket business yesterday?"

Pola paused in his work and gave Darek a long, thoughtful look. He glanced over his shoulder to see if Daxon or any of his men were around, then moved closer.

"It's curious," he said. "The other prisoners say that the Blues arrived the same day I did. They've been wondering where they came from. There haven't been any Blues here in the stockyard for many years. The Kradens don't usually raise them, because they're so large and fierce. The Red Fangs have a hard time killing them."

A door opened, and Darek turned to see the girl Rowena come in with a broom. She walked by, sweeping.

"Thrummm!" Darek sang out. The next thing he knew, he was dancing around the girl, butting her with his head.

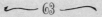

"What are you doing?" she cried. She whacked at him with her broom.

"Thrummm, thrummm," Darek sang. And then the little Blue was there, dancing and thrumming, too. Round and round the girl they both frolicked.

"Enough!" a voice boomed.

A whip lashed out and stung Darek with a blow on the back. Stunned, he found himself hoisted up, dangling in front of Daxon's eyes.

"What kind of foolishness is this?" the Master roared.

Darek shook his head hard.

"Um—I—I don't know," he stammered. "Something came over me. I'm sorry."

"You'll be sorry, all right," the Master said, "when you don't eat again tonight! Pola, tether that dragon in the pen. Wench! Back to the kitchen with you!"

Darek looked at the sad little dragon as Pola led it away. For an instant, something seemed to pass between them. It was too fast-moving, too vague to capture, but it felt strangely like a memory.

Darek felt himself blushing when the prisoners filed into his room that night. How could he explain his silly actions to Rowena?

"I'm sorry about today," he began.

"No need." Rowena gave him a strange look. "I understand."

"You do?"

She nodded. "I think so."

"Understand what?" Arnod asked.

Darek turned to him. "I think one of the Blue

dragons might hold the key to who we are," he whispered. "I've got to find a way to spend more time with him."

"But how could a dragon help us?" Arnod asked.

"I don't know," Darek said. "I just think he can."

"Yes." Rowena nodded. "Darek's right. I feel it too."

Arnod shrugged. "It won't be easy to arrange," he said. "And there may not be much time left."

"Time left?" Darek wrinkled his brow. "What do you mean?"

"The Kradens will probably feed him and the other Blues to the Fangs early, before they grow too big and strong."

"Then we have to start soon," Darek said. "Tonight, if possible."

Arnod sat back and chewed his lip thoughtfully. "We have passages all through the complex," he said. "But Daxon posts a watch on the nursery and stables at night. It would be too dangerous to go there."

"There must be somewhere else," Darek said.

"There's the granary, next to the nursery," Arnod said. "We may be able to sneak the Blue in there. It's dangerous, though. Very dangerous. If the creature makes a noise—if you are discovered—the passages, everything will be uncovered. We could all be fed to the Fangs."

Darek shivered, but then he took a deep breath and squared his shoulders. "You speak longingly of freedom," he said, "but you will never taste it unless you make it happen. And you cannot make it happen without taking risks. I, for one, would rather die than spend the rest of my life a prisoner." He looked around the circle of faces. "What about you?"

Pola leaned forward quickly and clapped a hand on Darek's knee. "I'm with you, my friend," he said.

Rowena nodded. "I, too."

Arnod and the others exchanged glances, then one by one they nodded as well. Arnod stretched his right arm out toward the center of the circle, and the others did the same. Darek placed his hand on top.

"To freedom!" he said.

9

"*THRUMMM, THRUMMM, THRUMMM,*"
the dragonling sang softly.

Darek stroked its head and looked deep into
its eyes. "Do you know me, young one?" he asked.
"Have we been friends in another place?"

Warm feelings flowed into Darek's mind. Joy,
love—emotions strangely out of place in this cold,
dark granary. But that was all he seemed to get
from the dragon—just feelings.

Though he was disappointed, Darek murmured gently and stroked the little beast's blue-scaled back. When his hand reached the wing bindings, he felt something sticky and wet. He pulled his hand away and looked at it.

Blood.

"Poor thing," he said. "Why didn't you let us know your bindings were cutting you? Here, let me help."

Carefully Darek unwound the bindings until the little creature fluttered its wings.

"*Thrummm, thrummm,*" it cried again. In its joy, it fluttered right up off the floor.

"Shush," Darek said, laughing softly. Then, as he watched the beast flutter around the room, an idea slowly came to him. If he brought the dragonling here every night and let him exercise his wings, he might still be able to fly. And if he could fly, then somehow, someday, Darek might be able to ride him back to where he came from. Back to . . . "Home," Darek whispered, looking deeply into the dragon's eyes again. "Do you want to take me *home*?"

Suddenly an image sprang into Darek's mind, an image that the dragonling seemed to be sending. It was a lovely farmhouse with rolling green pastures around it. There was a barn, too, filled with bales of sweet-smelling zorgrass. Outside, in the paddock, a boy was playing with a little Blue dragon. When the boy called out the beast's name, Darek's breath caught in his throat.

"Zantor," he whispered, still gazing into the dragon's eyes. "That's your name! And that's our home, yours and mine, isn't it?"

The little forked tongue flicked out and planted a kiss on his cheek. *"Thrummm,"* Zantor sang. *"Thrummm, thrummm, thrummm."*

Darek smiled and rubbed the dragon's nubby head. "Pola," he said. "Tell me about Pola."

Images filled Darek's head again, pictures of Darek, Zantor, and Pola. First they were romping through fields, then splashing in a brook. Lastly he saw the three of them lazing in front of a crackling fire.

"So, he's my best friend," Darek said. "No wonder I like him so well. And what of the girl Rowena?"

Warm, loving feelings flooded through Darek. He felt the touch of gentle hands and saw beautiful eyes staring into his. For a moment, he could hardly breathe. Then he laughed softly.

"She's very special to you, isn't she, Zantor?" he whispered.

"*Thrummm,*" Zantor sang.

The long days of toil passed quickly for Darek. He worked harder than any of the other prisoners, and muscles began to bulge on his back and arms. Whenever Daxon sent for him or assigned him a new task, he went out of his way to please. He wanted Daxon to be happy, to enjoy every drop of his evening slog, and to stay far away from the granary at night.

Darek and his friends had begun training Zantor and some of the other dragons to fly with riders on their backs. Little by little, Zantor was giving Darek and Rowena and Pola their memories back. They, in turn, shared what they learned with the others. There were still many gaps, but this much they knew: Zoriak *was* real, a beautiful green place, with sparkling clear air. Freedom waited there, and their families, too, if only they could figure out how to return. Exactly where Zoriak was, they still didn't know. But Darek was confident that Zantor would be able to remember and lead them there.

Darek, Pola, Rowena, Arnod, and the others had fashioned saddles and bridles out of bits of cloth and leather. Working together each night, they soon became friends. The dragons were growing bigger every day. Before long, they would all make their escape.

There was still the dragonsbreath to contend with, of course. But Darek, Pola, and Rowena knew they had come through it once without losing their wits, so there had to be a chance of doing it again. It was only a chance, of course, but it was a chance they were willing to take.

10

DAREK HAD BEEN ASSIGNED TO THE
stalls instead of the nursery all morning. At lunch-
time, he looked up to see Pola running toward
him. He was pale and out of breath.

"What is it?" Darek asked. "What's wrong?"

Pola looked around nervously. "The Blues!"
he whispered. "They took one of them early this
morning!"

"What?" Darek felt the blood draining from his face. "Which one?"

"Leezin, the one Arnod was training. She's . . . she's dead by now, fed to the Red Fangs."

Tears sprang to Darek's eyes. Gentle Leezin—dead?

"They could take the others as soon as tomorrow!" Pola warned.

Darek stared down at the floor, and his feet blurred through his tears. Zantor—fed to the Red Fangs tomorrow! He could not bear to think of it. Then he realized something else. Everything they had worked for, everything they had planned, would all be gone without the dragons. He sucked in a deep breath and looked up again.

"We must leave tonight," he said.

Pola's eyes widened. "Tonight! But the dragons aren't strong enough," he said. "We'll never make it."

"Then we'll die trying," Darek said.

It was decided that only Darek, Pola, and Rowena would go. Their Blues were bigger and stronger than the other dragons and stood a chance of success. Trying to fly the smaller dragons while they were still so young would have been much too dangerous for riders and dragons alike.

Well after dark, Darek, Pola, and Rowena stood in a circle in the granary with the others. They reached their hands into the center.

"We will be back, my friends," Darek said.

"We will be waiting," Arnod replied.

"Train as many dragons as you can," Darek said. "They will be useful when the time comes."

Arnod and the others nodded.

Darek felt tears start behind his eyes. He and his friends were being brave, but in their hearts they knew they might never see one another again. It would be a miracle if the escape succeeded, and whatever the result, it would surely bring the wrath of Zahr down on those who remained behind. But it did no good to dwell on such things. They had no choice.

"The alarms will sound as soon as the doors open," Arnod warned. "Your only hope will be to get a strong head start before they get the Fangs into the air."

"We will," Darek assured him. He mounted Zantor, and Pola and Rowena mounted the two remaining Blues.

"Now!" he commanded Arnod.

Arnod and the others pulled back the granary doors. Immediately the piercing shriek of a siren split the air. Darek shouted the flight command, and the three dragons pushed off with their powerful legs, pumping their small wings mightily. The ground began to fall away beneath them.

"We're going to make it!" Pola shouted.

"Yes!" Rowena cried out. "We're going home!"

Darek wasn't quite as certain. He could feel Zantor's heart pounding against his knees. He and the others were heavy burdens for dragons so young. Below them, Krad was springing to life. Men scurried everywhere. Arrows were shot into the air but fell far short of their marks. Before long, though, Darek heard the horrible screams of Red Fangs. He looked back and saw several beasts and riders in pursuit.

"Home, Zantor, home!" he cried. "Faster!"

Zantor pumped his wings harder, but arrows whizzed around them now. The Red Fangs were fast approaching. Soon they would be within flaming distance. Darek glanced from left to right. Pola and Rowena were still with him, and the mountains were drawing closer. If they could just make it into the thick of the mist, they would be safe. The Kradens could not pursue them there. But Zantor's heart was thumping rapidly now. How much longer could he endure?

Suddenly there was a burst of flame off to Darek's right. A Red Fang was gaining on him. The flame came again, closer. Darek cried out and dropped the reins as his sleeve caught fire.

"You okay?" Pola called.

"Yes!" Darek lurched wildly, trying to beat out the flames. He gripped Zantor's back with just his knees. Rowena flew in close and desperately tried to help him. The mist was thickening. Safety was so close!

"Go on!" Darek called to Rowena as he tried to shrug out of his burning shirt. "Whatever happens, just keep going!"

Then there was a searing pain in his leg. Darek stared mutely at the arrow shaft and the widening circle of red. Another arrow whizzed by, plunging into Zantor's neck. *"Eeeiiieee!"* Zantor screamed. And then they were falling. . . .

11

"WELL, WELL. GOOD MORNING."

Darek blinked to clear the haze from his eyes. A great fur-covered face stared down at him—a Kraden. He swallowed hard as the truth sank in. He had been captured again. He tried to move but winced in pain. Where was he? he wondered. He blinked again and looked around. He appeared to be in a cave of some sort, lit by torches on the walls.

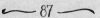

"Who are you?" he asked the Kraden. "Where am I?"

"I am Azzon," the man said, "the rightful King of Krad. You are in my chambers. The Zynots brought you here."

"Zynots?" Darek mumbled.

"The little creatures who inhabit these mountains," the man explained. "They tell me you did them a kindness in the past. They wished to repay it."

Azzon nodded at Darek's leg. Darek looked down and saw that it had been wrapped in a plaster and bandaged.

"I have no memory of Zynots," he said. "Nor do I think it a kindness to deliver me back into Kraden hands."

"We are not in Kraden hands," a voice said. "Azzon is a friend."

Darek turned to see Rowena ducking through a low door. Pola followed her into the room.

"What are you two doing here?" Darek cried.

"We came back when you fell," Pola said.

"You fools!" Darek shook his head. "I told you to keep going!"

"It is well that they did not," Azzon said, "or they would be witless by now."

"We've already been through the mountains once," Darek argued. "The dragonsbreath did not harm us."

"Your lungs were clean and strong then," Azzon said. "You have lived too long in Krad now. You would not have made it this time."

Darek turned back to Pola and Rowena. "Zantor?" he asked. "What of Zantor?"

Pola and Rowena exchanged troubled glances.

"We don't know," Pola said quietly. "He disappeared after you fell."

Darek was silent, remembering the arrow.

"We freed our dragons," Rowena said, "and sent them after him. They'll find him."

Darek bit his lip, close to tears. Poor Zantor. Even if the other dragons did find him, how could they help if he was hurt or dying?

12

AZZON SAT BACK IN HIS CHAIR AND puffed slowly on a long clay pipe.

"There is not much more to tell," he said. "Kradens have always known of the existence of Zoriak, but it never troubled us. The few Zorians who came over the mountains were easily dealt with. The dragonsbreath potion quickly robbed them of their memories. In time, our Zorian prisoners began to wonder if the old legends of Zoriak were even true."

"What about the Zynots?" Darek asked. "Who are they?"

Azzon laughed. "Your ancient kin," he said. "They are Zorians who lost their wits and their way in the Long Ago. In time, their bodies changed. Now they are prisoners of the mountain, able to breathe only dragonsbreath." Azzon pulled thoughtfully at the graying fur on his chin. "They are timid and foolish," he said, "but kind and good, too. I owe my life to them."

"Your life?" Rowena's brow wrinkled in disbelief. "How came the King of Krad to owe his life to Zynots?"

Azzon smiled sadly. "As you have seen," he said, "Kradens love blood sport, and I, their king, loved it better than any other. There was never a dragon fight bloody enough for me, a battle fierce enough, until the day my sons, Zahr and Rebbe, turned on each other. It was then, and only then, that I saw what I had done to them. I had raised them like Red Fangs, living to kill. When I tried to stop them from killing each other, they turned their fury on me."

Azzon took a long puff on his pipe and stared blankly at the walls. Darek swallowed hard and glanced at Pola and Rowena.

"I fled into these mountains, expecting to die," Azzon went on softly. "The Zynots found me and brought me here, to this cave beneath the mountains. The dragonsbreath cannot penetrate here. The Zynots have seen to my needs ever since, but it is a lonely life. They cannot tarry long in my world, nor I in theirs."

"Is there no way out?" Darek asked.

"Not for me," Azzon said. Then he leaned forward and rested his arms on his knees. "But perhaps for you. Before we speak of it, though, you must explain something to me."

"What is that?" Darek asked.

Azzon narrowed his eyes. "How did you get your memories back?"

Darek straightened in his seat. He dared not tell Azzon the truth. Who knew if Azzon could be trusted? He scrambled to come up with an answer that would satisfy Azzon without giving away the secret of Zantor's mind messages. What was it Azzon had said earlier? Something about a dragonsbreath potion?

"We didn't get our memories back," Darek

said quickly. "I . . . never really lost mine. I never drank the potion."

Azzon regarded him intently. "How can that be?"

Darek scrambled to think. His first memories of Krad were of a dark house, an old crone, and a guard. "The old woman gave me the potion," he explained, "but her house was dark and steamy. I tilted my head back and let it run out of the side of my mouth and down my neck. Then I pretended my memory was gone."

Azzon continued to stare hard at Darek. "How did you know the potion was meant to rob your memory?" he asked.

"The guard, Org, spoke of it."

After a time, Azzon nodded slowly. Then he rose and reached for a shelf on the wall. He took down a vial of green liquid and three small cups. Then he turned to face Darek and the others again.

"Be assured," he said. "*I* will not be as careless as Jazee."

13

"BUT WAIT!" DAREK JUMPED UP. "You said you were a friend! Why are you sending us back?"

"I'm not sending you back," Azzon said. "I'm sending you home."

"Home?" Darek sat down again with a thump.

"Home?" Pola and Rowena echoed.

"Yes." Azzon nodded. "There is a tunnel. An underground passage to Zoriak. I will take you there tonight. But you must go without your memories."

"But our friends . . . ," Pola started to protest.

"I cannot allow you to remember your friends," Azzon said. "You might try to help them."

"What's wrong with that?" Rowena asked. "Maybe we could help you, too."

Azzon shook his head. "If I wanted to help myself, I could go with you tonight," he said. "But I am old and wise. I know that things are not always as simple as they seem. Your world and mine are not ready to come together."

"Why not?" Darek asked. "Maybe we could make your world better."

"Better how?" Azzon asked. "By trying to destroy my sons? They may be cruel and evil, but they are still my sons. And what of the dragons of

Krad, the mighty Red Fangs? Would you kill them? Then you might as well kill the Zynots, for they will die anyway without the dragonsbreath. Have you the stomach for so much killing?"

Darek swallowed. He had no stomach for killing at all.

"Azzon is right," Rowena said sadly.

Pola nodded.

"But what of our friends?" Darek asked.

"If freedom means as much to your friends as it does to you," Azzon said, "they will find their own way."

14

DAREK, ROWENA, AND POLA STOOD
facing Azzon. The night air was soft and fragrant.
Zoriak's twin moons smiled down on them, wel-
coming them home. Azzon took out his vial.

"Drink," he commanded, pouring them each
a portion of the green liquid. "I have added
something to make you sleep. When you wake in
the morning, you will know your names, and you
will remember one another. But you will recall

nothing that has happened for at least two or three anums. . . ."

"Two or three anums!" Darek cried. "But . . . we won't even remember Zantor!"

"I'm sorry," Azzon said. "I cannot take the risk of allowing you to remember more. You must trust me. It is better this way." Then he smiled sadly and added, "Good life to you, my friends."

Darek, Pola, and Rowena slowly lifted their cups. "And to you, Azzon," they said softly. Then they tilted their heads and drank. Darek thought one last time about Arnod and the others.

"Farewell, my friends," he whispered. "Lord Eternal be with you." Then he thought about Zantor, and tears stung his eyes. "And with you, little friend," he whispered, "wherever you are."

✳ ✳ ✳

Darek opened his eyes and blinked. He was in a gently sloping field of zorgrass.

"What?" he whispered. "What am I doing here?" He rolled over and blinked again. "Pola? Rowena?" he said. "What are we all doing here?"

Pola and Rowena sat up and looked around.

"We're in the foothills of the Yellow Mountains!" Pola said.

"How did we get *here*?" Rowena asked.

"I don't know." Darek shook his head. "I do know one thing, though. Our parents are going to kill us."

"Uh-oh." Rowena pointed up at the sky. "You mean, if *they* don't kill us first!"

Three young Blue dragons were winging their way over the Yellow Mountains.

"Stay calm," Darek said. "Maybe they won't see us."

"They see us, all right!" Pola shouted. "Here they come!"

They all jumped to their feet, and Rowena and Pola started to run. But for some reason, Darek didn't. Instead he stood and watched the dragons dip lower, lower, until they landed right in front of him.

One of them, a male, stared at him with pain-filled eyes. *"Rrronk!"* he cried.

"Why, you're hurt!" Darek said. A broken arrow shaft protruded from the dragon's neck.

Darek approached carefully.

"Here," he said, grabbing the shaft. "Let me help." He pulled, and the arrow came out clean. The young dragon seemed tired but grateful. He laid his head gently on Darek's shoulder.

"Thrummm," he sang softly. *"Thrummm, thrummm, thrummm."*

"Why . . . they're friendly." Rowena cried out.

Darek turned to see her and Pola watching in amazement.

"Is that one all right?" Pola asked, approaching cautiously.

"I think so." Darek reached up and gently stroked the dragon's neck. "Poor thing. I wonder who shot him? This arrow isn't Zorian."

The little dragon pulled back. He tilted his head and looked deeply into Darek's eyes. For an instant, something seemed to pass between them, something too fast-moving, too vague to capture.

Something that felt strangely like a memory.

Turn the page for a peek
at the next book in the series:

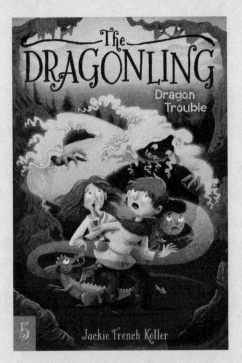

Dragon Trouble

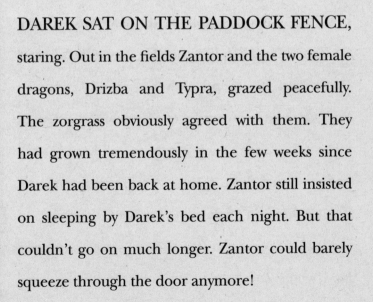

1

DAREK SAT ON THE PADDOCK FENCE, staring. Out in the fields Zantor and the two female dragons, Drizba and Typra, grazed peacefully. The zorgrass obviously agreed with them. They had grown tremendously in the few weeks since Darek had been back at home. Zantor still insisted on sleeping by Darek's bed each night. But that couldn't go on much longer. Zantor could barely squeeze through the door anymore!

Little by little, Darek was trying to piece together what had happened to him since Zantor came into his life. He and his friends Pola and Rowena had been to Krad and back. He knew that much. But someone, or something, had taken away their memories while they were there. Not just their memories of Krad, but their memories of several anums before, too. Darek's mother had been doing her best to fill in those anums for him.

Zantor was helping too. He was able to send Darek and his friend Rowena mind pictures of things he had heard and seen. These mind messages were giving them back memories of Krad. Darek hadn't shared these memories with his mother yet because he didn't want to worry her. They were too awful to share—scenes of a bleak, smoke-shrouded land, where Zorians were prisoners, and fierce, hairy

Kradens ruled. Darek swallowed hard. His father and brother were still in Krad somewhere, and Pola's and Rowena's fathers too. That is—if any of them were still alive.

Darek heard a shout and turned to see Pola and Rowena coming up the road.

"How's he doing?" asked Rowena. She hopped up on the fence and nodded toward the scar on Zantor's neck. Zantor and Darek had both been wounded by arrows in their escape from Krad.

"Good as new," said Darek. "Look at him."

The three friends watched as Zantor charged the other two dragons in a play battle. Drizba and Typra reared and screamed in mock terror. Darek, Pola, and Rowena laughed.

"How about you?" Pola asked then. "How's the leg coming along?"

Darek rubbed his thigh. "A little stiff still, but nothing I can't handle. Any further word on our punishment?"

"No." Rowena bit her lip. There was a law in Zoriac that anyone caught venturing into the Black Mountains was to be put to death. Pola did not need to worry. He had been carried into the mountains by accident. But Darek and Rowena had gone after him willingly. Under Zorian law, when a child under twelve broke the law, the child's father was made to suffer the punishment, even if that father was Chief Elder, like Rowena's father. But Darek's father and the Chief Elder were gone, along with Pola's father and Darek's brother. They had gone into the Black Mountains too, to search for the children. And they had not returned.

"It's all so confusing," Rowena went on.

"Mother says the elders can't decide what to do. I worry what will happen when our fathers get back, though. Zarnak, the acting chief, seems very fond of that crown on his head. I think he will be all too glad of a reason to put my father to death."

Pola shook his head firmly. "Your father has too many friends on the Council," he said to Rowena. "And Darek, your father is one of the most respected men in the village. Don't worry about that old law. It was only made to scare Zorians away from the Black Mountains for their own safety."

"That's not quite true," said Rowena. "It was also meant to prevent Zorians from going over the mountains and provoking the Kradens, *if* they in fact existed."

"*Thrummm, thrummm, thrummm!*" The young dragons had noticed the children and came loping over. They stuck their heads over the fence to be petted.

"Here," Darek said, pulling some sugar cubes from his jerkin pocket. He handed a few to Pola and Rowena. "Zantor reminded me yesterday that he loves these."

The three children held out the cubes and, *thwippp, thwippp, thwippp!* The dragons gobbled them eagerly.

"Have you gotten any more mind messages from Zantor?" Rowena asked Darek as they watched the dragons munch.

"Shush!" Darek glanced back toward the house. "I don't think my mother, or anyone else, should know what we've found out about Krad until we can figure a way to get our fathers back."

"Why?" asked Rowena.

"Because I don't trust Zarnak. As far as I'm concerned, the less he knows, the better."

Rowena and Pola nodded their agreement.

"The last memory I can get from Zantor," Darek went on, "is when the arrow struck my leg. But . . . how did we get home? We made it through the mists *somehow*."

Pola and Rowena nodded again. They had learned from Zantor's mind messages that the mists in the Black Mountains were poisonous. The poison was deadly to Kradens and robbed Zorians of their minds.

"We've *got* to find out how we did it," said Darek.

"Why?" asked Pola. "What are you planning?"

Darek glanced toward the house and then lowered his voice. "I'm going back," he said.

A wry smile slowly curled Pola's lips. "When do we leave?" he asked.

"I didn't say *we*," said Darek. "I said *me*. I'm already in trouble. You're not."

Pola bristled. "Oh, right," he said, "like I'd ever let you go alone. My father's over there too, don't forget."

"And mine!" Rowena put in.

Both boys turned to look at her. "You're not suggesting we take *you* back there?" said Darek. "It's too dangerous!"

Rowena crossed her arms over her chest and narrowed her eyes. "Nobody *takes* me anywhere," she said. "I go where I *please*. And *if* I please to go with you, I *will*. Just like I did last time."

"*Rrronk!*" came a sudden cry. The young dragons had finished the sugar cubes and gone back to their games. Apparently Zantor had started playing a little too rough, knocking Drizba down. As Darek, Pola, and Rowena watched, Drizba got to her feet, threw back her head, and spread her wings.

"*Grrrawwk!*" she screamed in a *very* convincing imitation of an angry, full-grown Blue.

"*Rrronk, rrronk!*" cried Zantor. He barreled across the field, leapt the fence in a single bound, and dove for cover behind Darek.

"Wow," said Darek, "she's pretty impressive when she gets mad. I thought for a minute she was going to breathe fire."

"Who?" asked Pola, grinning widely, "Drizba, or Rowena?"

2

"MOTHER?" DAREK CALLED.

"Up here," Alayah answered.

Darek climbed the narrow, winding staircase to the garret.

"Rrronk," cried Zantor. Darek looked back and saw him wedged in the doorway. The garret stairs were too narrow for him.

"Silly dragon," said Darek. He went back down and pushed Zantor free. "Just wait here," he said.

"I'll only be a moment." Zantor's head sagged. He rested his chin on one of the lower steps and watched sadly as Darek climbed up, out of his reach.

Alayah was just closing an old chest as Darek entered the garret. She dabbed quickly at her eyes with her apron.

"What are you doing?" Darek asked.

"Nothing," she said, "just . . ." Her voice trailed off.

Darek walked over and crouched down beside her. "What's in here?" he asked. Before his mother could answer, he lifted the lid and looked in. The chest was full of yellowed letters and baby clothes. Some of his father's old uniforms, medals, and archery trophies were there too.

"Just memories," Darek's mother said softly.

Darek lifted out one of the trophies and sat

with it on his lap. He thought of the days when he and Clep were small. Often, in the evenings, after supper, his father would set a target up beyond the barn and let them practice with his great bow. At first Darek had been too small even to bend the string, but his father would twine his fingers through Darek's and help him pull.

"You did it!" Clep would cry when the arrow found its mark. Then Darek would feel proud, even though he knew he couldn't have done it without his father.

Tears sprang to Darek's eyes. How he missed his father and brother.